UNICORN

thinks he's pretty great

Bob Shea

Disney · Hyperion Books/New York

For information address Disney • Hyperion Books,
114 Fifth Avenue, New York, New York 10011-5690.

First Edition
10 9 8 7 6 5 4 3 2 1
H106-9555-5-13046
Printed in Malaysia

Reinforced binding

Library of Congress Cataloging-in-Publication Data

Shea, Bob.
Unicorn thinks he's pretty great / by Bob Shea.—First edition.
    pages   cm
Summary: Envy turns to admiration and finally friendship for Goat and
Unicorn.
ISBN 978-1-4231-5952-0
[1. Unicorns—Fiction. 2. Goats—Fiction. 3. Envy—Fiction. 4. Friendship—
Fiction.] I. Title. II. Title: Unicorn thinks he is pretty great.
PZ7.S53743Un 2013   [E]—dc23   2012047987

Visit www.disneyhyperionbooks.com

For Ryan and his magical mom

Things are a lot different around here
since that Unicorn moved in.

I thought I was pretty cool when
I rode my bike to school.

Until that **show-off** went flying by!

Or the time I made marshmallow squares
that almost came out right.

He made it **rain cupcakes!**

Then, at the big talent show,
I was dropping my signature
dance moves ...

when he steps up with some serious prancing and wins first prize!

That's not all!
It gets much, much worse!
Check out this great magic trick
that I totally invented....

While your eyes were closed,
I pulled this quarter out
from behind your ear!

Nice, right?

Well, when I get to school to try it out,
he's turning stuff into gold!

I can't follow that!

BINK!

Dopey Unicorn!

Thinks he's so great!

How can anyone be friends

with that guy?!

Look at me! I'm Unicorn!

I think I'm so-o-o cool!

Blah, blah, blah,

blah, blah...

Well, this goat's not buying it.
Great, here he comes.

What is that
heavenly
smell?!

Goat-cheese pizza.

I'm a goat.

What?!
Goats have cheese?
Unicorns don't have cheese.
May I try?

This cheese is **fan-tas-tic!** So creamy and delicious!

It's also good smeared
on a tin can or sprinkled
on some garbage.

Lucky!
I can only eat glitter and rainbows.
Darn my sensitive stomach!

Whoa!

What is up with your hooves?

Those things are
out of control!

Oh, these?

These bad boys
are "cloven."
It means they're
split at the end.

They let me stand on **steep** hills or climb to the **tops** of mountains.

Oh, man!

I can't stand there or climb those!

Stupid regular hooves!

Don't be so hard on yourself!
Just look at your fantastic horn.

That thing is nuts!

Eh, it's just for show.

All it's good for is pointing.

I can't play soccer.
One head butt and it's game over!

Pain-in-the-neck horn!

Not you, though.
I bet those awesome horns
are perfect for soccer!

I have an idea...
With your magic and
my awesome-ness ...

we'd be an unstoppable team!

Sure!

Or we can go to the park and play.

You know something, Unicorn?

I had a feeling we'd be friends.